I Like You
the Best

In memory of Brian Anson, friend, artist, and storyteller.

I LIKE YOU THE BEST by Carol Thompson was first published in Australia in 2010
by Little Hare Books, an imprint of Hardie Grant Egmont,
under the title *CHILL*. North American rights arranged through
Australian Licensing Corporation and Nancy Gallt.

First published in the United States by Holiday House, Inc. in 2011.
All Rights Reserved
HOLIDAY HOUSE is registered in the U.S. Patent and Trademark Office.
The text typefaces are Handwriter and Postcard.
Printed and Bound in October 2010 through Phoenix Offset in Shen Zhen,
Guangdong Province, China.
www.holidayhouse.com
First American Edition
1 3 5 7 9 10 8 6 4 2

Library of Congress Cataloging-in-Publication Data

Thompson, Carol.
I like you the best / by Carol Thompson. — 1st American ed.
p. cm.
Summary: Dolly the pig and Jack Rabbit are best friends, even after they have a fight.
ISBN 978-0-8234-2341-5 (hardcover)
[1. Best friends—Fiction. 2. Friendship—Fiction. 3. Pigs—Fiction. 4. Rabbits—Fiction.]
I. Title.
PZ7.T371423Ial 2011
[E]—dc22
2010030747

I Like You the Best

Carol Thompson

Holiday House / New York

Dolly likes to play on her own.

Dum-di-dum-di-dum!

Especially the mirror game.

But some games are not much fun all alone.

Then . . .

along comes Jack Rabbit,

Dolly's best friend in all the world.

Some days Jack and Dolly
are quiet together.
They go to their Best Place
and watch the clouds.

Or listen to their favorite music.

Some days they race around so fast

and play so hard,

all they can do is . . .

One day when Dolly went to visit
Jack, he was wearing a beret.

Jack painted a big circle.
And then some smaller circles.
Dolly painted some long, wobbly lines.

Dolly looked at Jack's picture.

Jack looked at Dolly's picture.

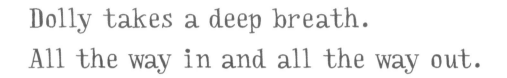

Dolly takes a deep breath.
All the way in and all the way out.

Dolly takes a
lovely warm bath.
She closes her
eyes and thinks
of something she
likes a lot.

Jack counts slowly up to ten,
and back down again.
And up again!

He closes his
eyes and thinks
of something he
likes a lot.

The next day . . .

Dolly goes to her Best Place.

Jack goes to his Best Place.